For my Parents

Scholastic Children's Books,
Scholastic Publications Ltd,
7-9 Pratt Street, London NW1 0AE, UK

Scholastic Inc.,
555 Broadway, New York, NY 10012-3999, USA

Scholastic Canada Ltd,
123 Newkirk Road, Richmond Hill,
Ontario, Canada L4C 3G5

Ashton Scholastic Pty Ltd,
PO Box 579, Gosford, New South Wales,
Australia

Ashton Scholastic Ltd,
Private Bag 92801, Penrose, Auckland,
New Zealand

First published in hardback by Scholastic Publications Ltd, 1993
This edition published 1995

Copyright © Helen Cooper, 1993

ISBN: 0 590 55829 3

Typeset by Rapid Reprographics
Printed in Belgium by Proost Book Production

THE
HOUSE CAT

Written and illustrated by
Helen Cooper

This is Tom-Cat's house.
Two families live here,
one upstairs,
one downstairs,
but Tom-Cat
lives in all the house,
for he is the House-Cat.

The Spode-Fawcetts live
downstairs, and think that
Tom-Cat belongs to them.
They want a pet to
match the carpet.
Tom-Cat matches beautifully.
But they're always cross about
hair on the chairs.
They are ungrateful,
bad tempered.
So Tom-Cat lives in all the house,
for he is the House-Cat.

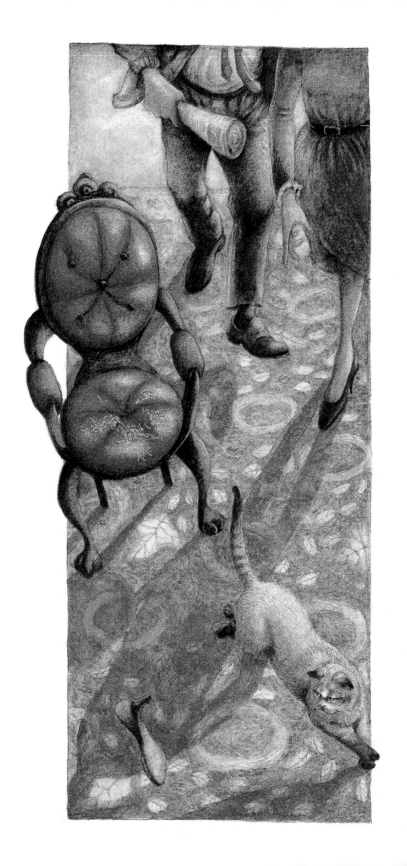

Tom-Cat knows
it's warmer upstairs...
and he's allowed
on the furniture there.
Jennifer's stroking is very good.
"Quite right too!" he purrs,
"for I am the House-Cat."

But what's all this?
Two men are putting the
downstairs furniture into
a big green lorry.
This is not good!
Tom-Cat hurries to investigate,
for he is the House-Cat.

"I will spit and I will claw!" growls Tom-Cat when he sees what's going on. But Mrs Spode-Fawcett picks him up, and squashes him into a cardboard cage. "You can't do this to me!" he rages, "I am the House-Cat."

The Spode-Fawcetts are moving house.
They are taking Tom-Cat with them.
But they have not asked his permission about anything!
"Miaoowieeeooooweeooowww" he wails,
"what's happening!"

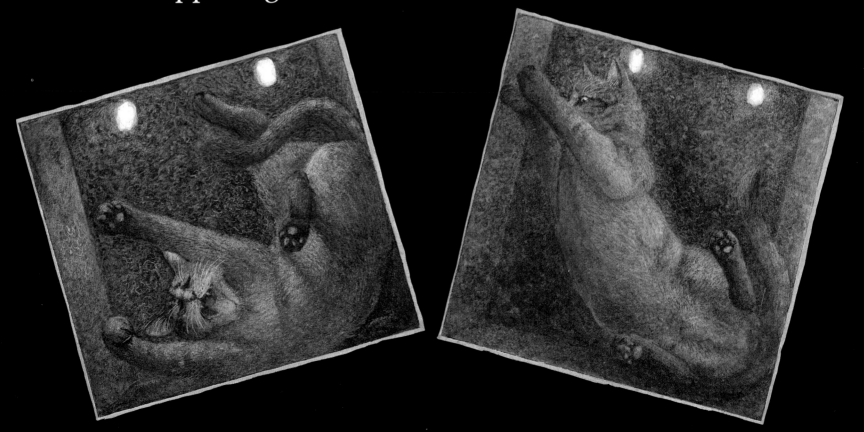

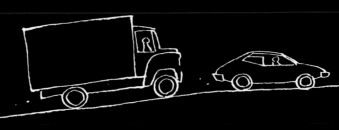

The box is hard,
his claws hurt.
Then...

...he smells
something good.

...he sees
great white birds.

...he hears
a horrid noisy
highway.

. . . he senses
DOGS!

...he knows
this is not his house.

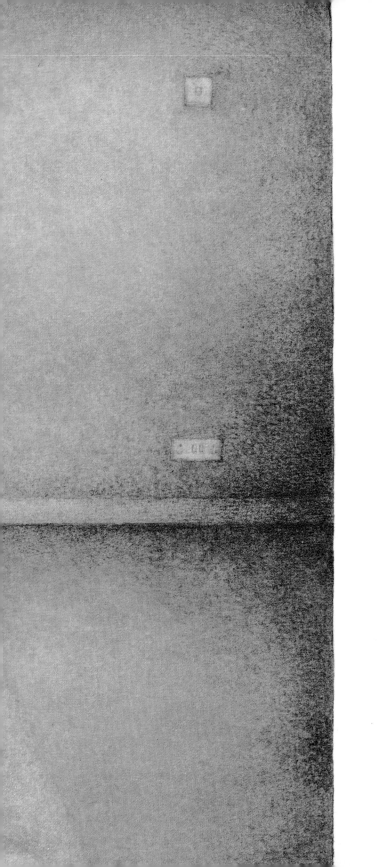

Tom-Cat's box is opened.
He stretches,
he sniffs...
This is not his house,
not his room,
not his carpet,
he will scratch it.

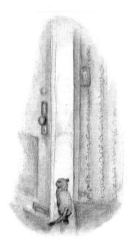

"That animal will have to go!"
snarls Mr Spode-Fawcett when
he sees the mess.
Mrs Spode-Fawcett agrees.
"Yes, he really doesn't match our
new carpet. Perhaps a poodle
would be better instead."
They bustle around in their new
home, they have no time for cats.
"This is not my house!" he says,
"I will go home…"

...and somehow, in his head he knows the way.

He must go quickly,
no time for play.

Quick...past the dogs!

Cat-quick!

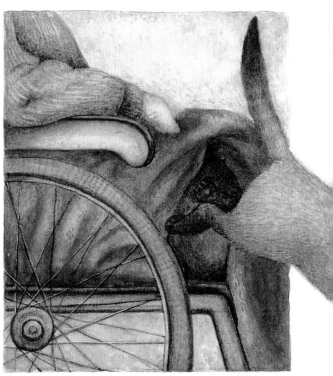

Quick!
over the road.
Quick!
over the wall.
Cat-quick!

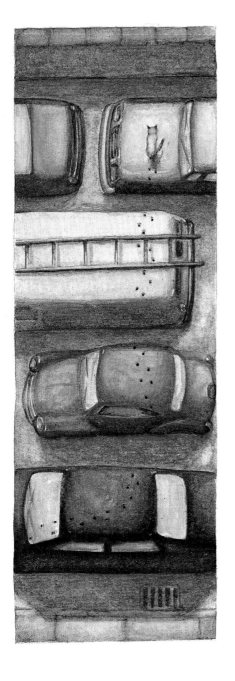

But wait...there are
no stepping stones,
no path,
no cat-walk.
And where are the
great white birds?

They're here.
They don't like cats!

Tom-Cat must swim.
He hates it.
He finds a cat-raft.
He sits,
and spins,
and shivers
in the cold wind.
He is lost.

But here comes a boat.
People reach over and
rescue him.
They love him,
and wonder if he'll be
their Boat-Cat and
live in their cabin.

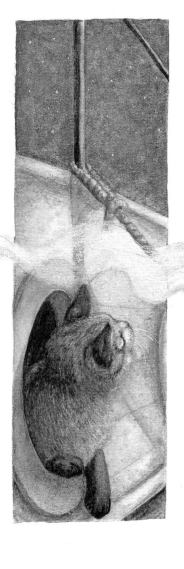

"But I am a House-Cat,
not a Boat-Cat," he says,
sniffing the night air.
He sniffs again,
sniffs a whiff
of something good.
He knows that smell!

Now he's off
tail up,
ears back,
he's Hunting-Cat,
he's Tracking-Cat.
Now he knows the way...

Home!

Jennifer thinks he's come back to be her cat.
A new family has moved in downstairs, and
they think that Tom-Cat is going to be their cat.
But Tom-Cat lives in all the house...

... for
he is the
House-Cat.